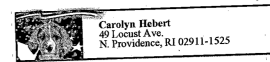

P9-DBX-819

MY RIVER

by Shari Halpern

Macmillan Publishing Company   New York

Maxwell Macmillan Canada   Toronto

Maxwell Macmillan International   New York   Oxford   Singapore   Sydney

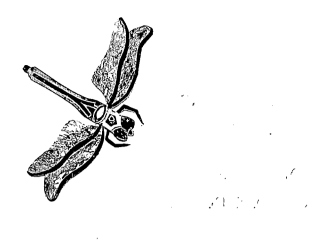

For their help with this book, I would like to thank John Cronin, Alan Reingold, Judy Sue Goodwin-Sturges, Beverly Reingold, Jean Krulis, James P. Rod, and Lynne O'Malley.

For specific information about how to help our rivers, contact: Riverkeeper, P.O. Box 130, Garrison, N.Y. 10524.

1   3   5   7   9   10   8   6   4   2

Library of Congress Cataloging-in-Publication Data
Halpern, Shari. My river / by Shari Halpern. — 1st ed.   p.   cm. Summary: Frogs, fish, a turtle, and other animals who live in or around a river state their need for the river, making a plea for protecting this natural resource. ISBN 0-02-741980-0 [1. Stream animals—Fiction.]   I. Title.
PZ7.H1667My   1992   [E]—dc20   91-33582

For Maw, Pop, and Maura,
who are pleased and proud

and for Jaclyn,
who would have been

Whose river is this?

It's my river.

It's our river.

It's everyone's river!

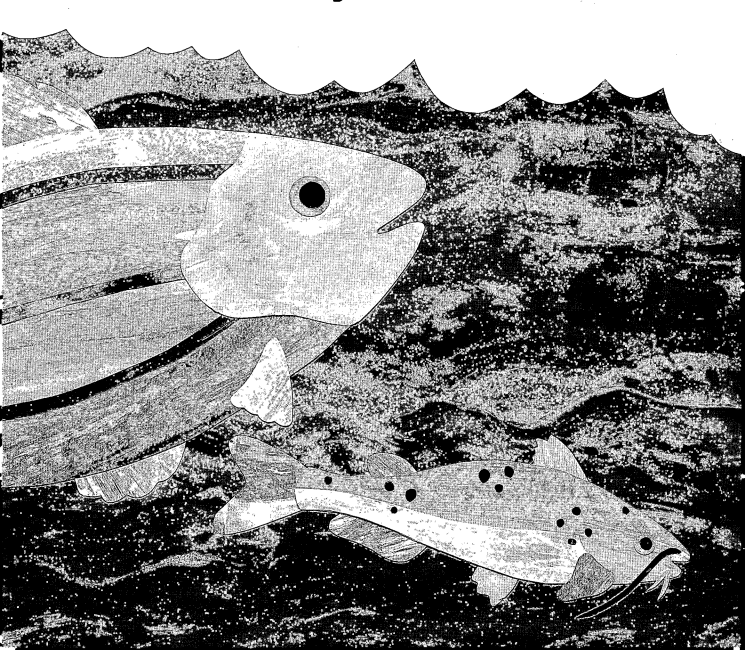

This is my home.

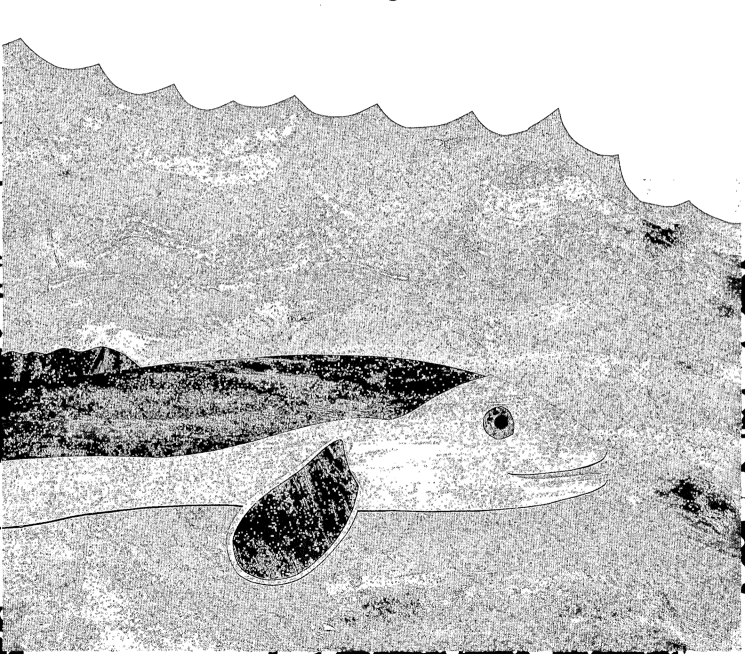

We live here, too.

I was born here.

This is where we grow.

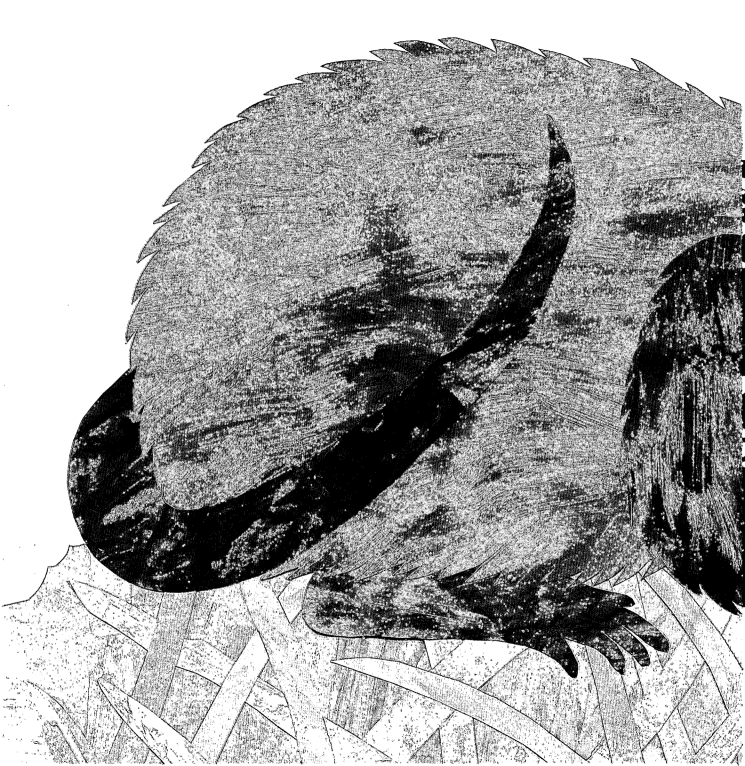

I need the river.

So do we.

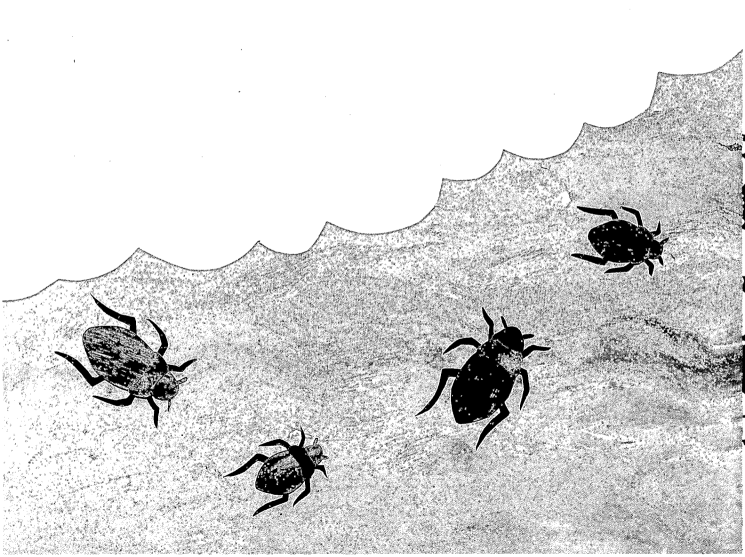

We *all* need the river!

This river is mine.

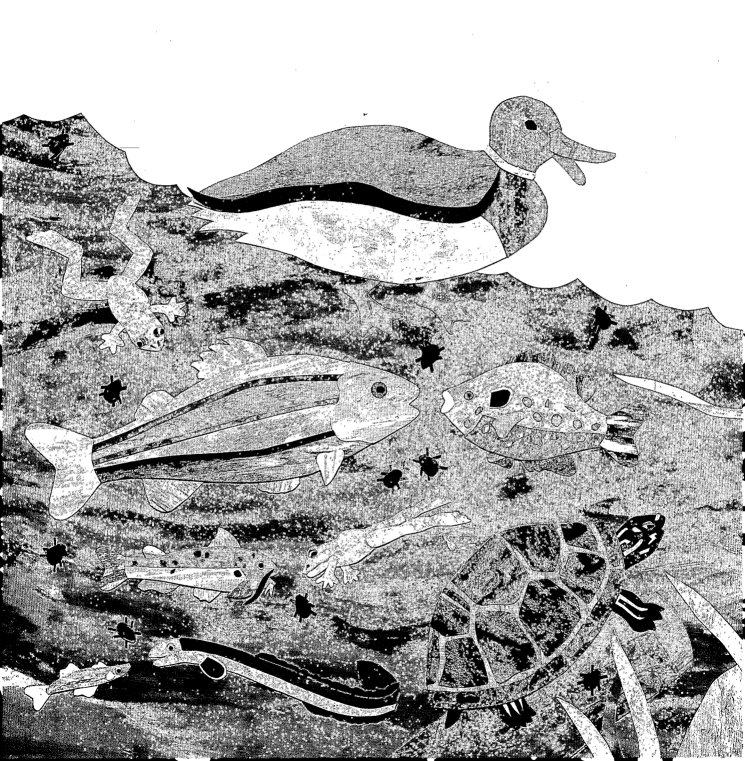

Whose river is it?

It's *everyone's* river!

 turtle

 vegetation

 frog

 muskrat

 fish

 water beetle

 eel

 duck

 salamander

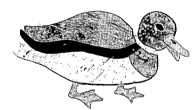 crayfish

 dragonfly

 children